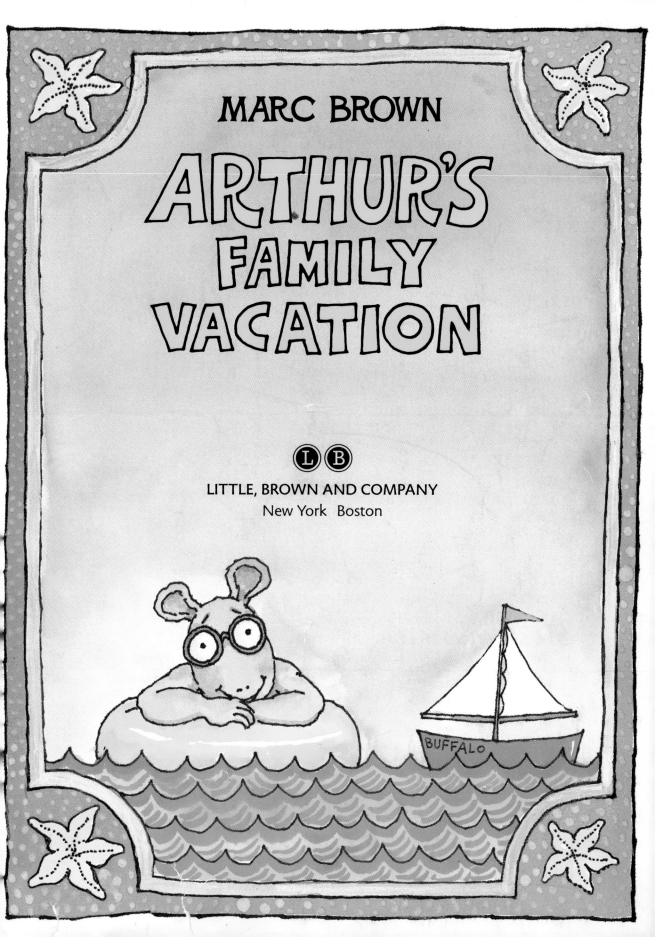

MARC BROWN

ARTHUR'S FAMILY VACATION

L **B**

LITTLE, BROWN AND COMPANY

New York Boston

For Melanie Kroupa,
who really needs one!

Little, Brown and Company
Hachette Book Group
237 Park Avenue, New York, NY 10017
Visit our website at www.lb-kids.com

Little, Brown and Company is a division of Hachette Book Group, Inc.
The Little, Brown name and logo are trademarks of Hachette Book Group, Inc.

First Revised Edition: April 2011
First published in hardcover in May 1993 by Little, Brown and Company

Arthur® is a registered trademark of Marc Brown.

Library of Congress Cataloging-in-Publication Data

Brown, Marc Tolon.
    Arthur's family vacation / Marc Brown.—1st ed.
        p. cm.
Summary: Arthur is unhappy about going on vacation with his family, but he shows them how to make the best of a bad situation when they end up stuck in a motel because of rain.
ISBN 978-0-316-11312-0 (hc) / ISBN 978-0-316-10958-1 (pb)
[1. Vacations—Fiction. 2. Family life—Fiction. 3. Animals—Fiction.] I. Title
PZ7.B8168APL 1993 92-26650

20 19

SC

Printed in China

It was Arthur's last day of school.
Mr. Ratburn gave the class a surprise spelling test.
All the other classes were having parties.
"Finally, the moment you've all been waiting for,"
said Mr. Ratburn. "Report cards and . . ."

". . . school's out!"

Everyone cheered.

"I can't wait for baseball practice to start," said Francine.

"I'm taking a college computer course," the Brain announced.

"I'll really miss you at Camp Meadowcroak this year, Arthur," Buster said.

"I wish I didn't have to go on vacation with my family," said Arthur. "There'll be nothing to do and no one to do it with."

"You'll have D.W., " Buster said, smiling. "For a whole week."

"Don't remind me," said Arthur.

Arthur's family spent that night packing.
"I wish I could take my dollhouse," said D.W.
"I wish Buster could come," said Arthur.
"This is a *family* vacation," said Mother.
"All we need for fun is each other," said Father.
"Let's take my swing set," said D.W. "We can all use that."

"Well, we're all packed," Father said the next morning.
"Where's Arthur?"
"He's on the phone with Buster," said Mother.
"For the hundredth time," D.W. added.
"Before we leave," said Father, "does anyone need to use the bathroom?"
"This is your last chance," said Mother.
"Don't look at me!" said D.W.

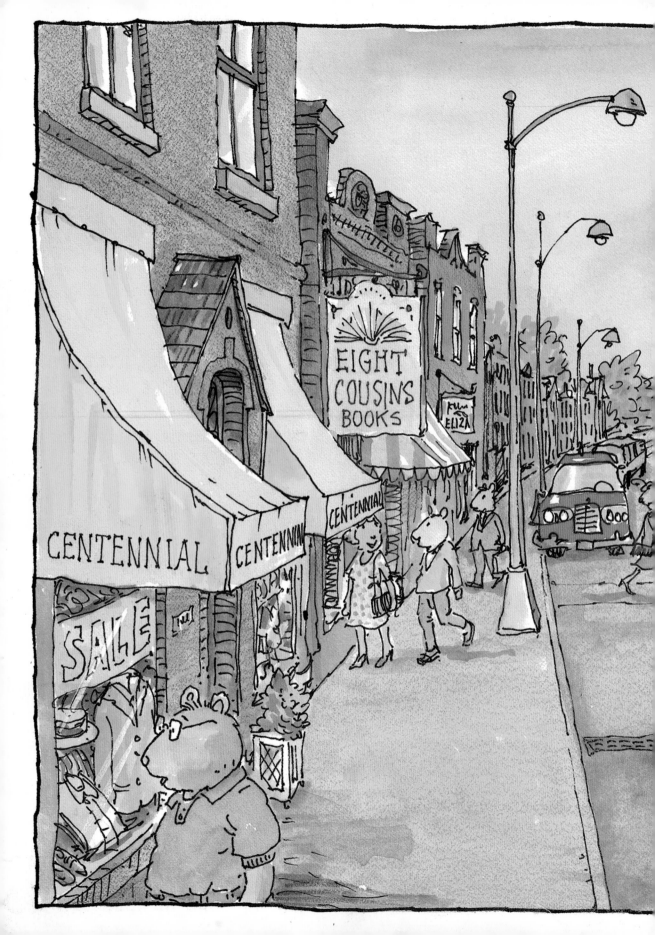

"On our way at last." Mother smiled. "A whole week of no cooking!"

"And no dishes," said Father.

"A whole week without my best friend in the whole wide world," moaned Arthur.

"Once you're at the beach, you'll feel better," Father said.

"Are we there yet?" asked D.W. "I have to go to the bathroom."

Arthur spent the rest of the trip thinking about how much fun Buster must be having at camp.

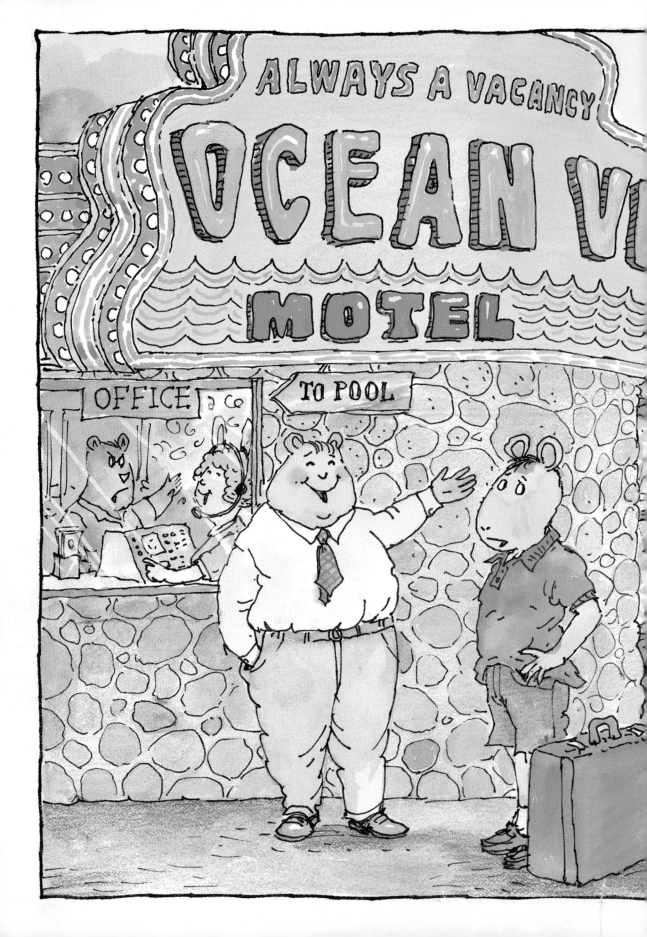

"We're here!" said Mother.

"Welcome to the Ocean View," said the manager.

"Where's the ocean?" asked Father.

"Just across the highway behind that shopping center."
The manager pointed. "But there's a pool right here."

"Well, I guess I'll go swimming," said Arthur.

"Me, too," said D.W. "Wait for me!"

"Let's see our room first," said Mother.

"You mean we all have to stay in this puny little room?" asked D.W.

"Don't worry," said Mother. "We'll only be sleeping here."

"If you want to swim," said Arthur, "hurry up and get your suit on."

"We have the whole pool to ourselves," said Arthur.
"It's a good thing, too," said D.W. "Our bathtub is
bigger than this!"

That night at dinner, everyone ordered lobster.
"Buster loves lobster!" said Arthur.
"*This* is lobster?" said D.W. "I want a hot dog."

"Can we go to the beach tomorrow?" Arthur asked.
"Good idea!" said Father. "I'm sure the rain will stop
by then."

"No beach today!" D.W. announced the next morning.
"I had a dream about Buster," said Arthur.
"Why don't you write him a postcard?" Mother
suggested.
"Why don't we all write postcards?" said Father.
"But what do we write about?" said D.W. "We haven't
done anything yet!"

Dear Buster,
I bet you're having fun at camp. I wish I were there.
Your best friend,
Arthur

POST CARD

Buster
Camp Meadowcroak

PLACE STAMP HERE

Dear Grandma Thora,
You were smart to stay home!
xxxoxoxo
Love,
D.W. xxxooootxoxxxo

POST CARD

PLACE STAMP HERE

Grandma Thora
47 Oakmont St.

"What do we do now?" said D.W. "This vacation is a disaster."

At camp there's always something fun to do, thought Arthur. Even on rainy days.

"That's it!" he said. "I'm taking us on a field trip."

"I never heard of a *cow* festival," D.W. said. "But at least it's more fun than our motel room."

"Say 'cheese,'" said Father.

"Let's hurry or we'll miss the milking contest," said Arthur.

For the next few days, it rained and rained, but Arthur didn't mind. He was too busy planning new places to go. He forgot all about missing Buster.

On Wednesday, they went to Gatorville.
"At least the alligators get to swim," said D.W.

ctory,

"I never realized there are so many fun things to do in the rain," said Father.

"I want to plan a field trip, too," said D.W. "To the movies."

But when they got there, D.W. was too scared to watch.
"I thought it was a movie about fish," she whispered.

Finally, on Friday, their last day, the sun came out.
"What a day!" said Father.
"Just glorious!" said Mother.
Even D.W. was having fun.

No one wanted to leave, but the next day, they packed up
and headed home.
"We're almost there," said Mother.
"Phew!" said D.W. "I really have to go to the bathroom."
"Oh, boy," said Arthur, "I can't wait to see Buster."

As soon as they got home, the doorbell rang.
It was Buster.
"Camp was fun, but I missed you," he said to Arthur.
"How was your vacation? How did you and D.W. get
along?"
"Great!" said Arthur. "Take a look."

"Wow!" said Buster. "You really did have a great time."